This book belongs to:

Good as Gold

Disney's Out & About With Pooh
A Grow and Learn Library

Published by Advance Publishers
© 1996 Disney Enterprises, Inc.
Based on the Pooh stories by A. A. Milne © The Pooh Properties Trust.

Written by Ann Braybrooks
Illustrated by Arkadia Illustration Ltd.
Designed by Vickey Bolling
Produced by Bumpy Slide Books

ISBN:1-885222-55-6
10 9 8 7 6 5 4 3 2 1

One drizzly day, Winnie the Pooh decided to stay inside and count his honey pots. "I know I had three pots of honey yesterday," he said to himself, "so I should have three pots of honey today."

Pooh opened his cupboard and counted slowly. "One, two," he said out loud.

"Two?" Pooh repeated, scratching his head. "Oh, bother! I seem to be missing number three. I wonder where it could be?"

Just then, Roo hopped through the door. "Come and
see the rainbow, Pooh!" the little kangaroo called, hopping
up and down.

Pooh forgot all about his missing honey pot and followed his friend outside. There he found Owl and Tigger gazing up at the sky.

Owl said, "Did I ever tell you what my Uncle Midas said about rainbows? He said there's a pot of gold at the end of every one!"

"What's gold?" Roo asked.

"Gold is something valuable, Roo," Owl explained. "Something anyone would like to have a lot of."

"Like honey?" Pooh said hopefully.

"Not exactly," Owl replied, puffing out his chest. "Gold is a shiny, yellowish—"

"That sounds like honey," Pooh interrupted.

"Well, it's not!" said Owl, becoming annoyed.

"I'm sorry, Pooh," said Owl, for he remembered that Pooh, being a bear of very little brain, sometimes needed extra help understanding things. "Let me explain it this way," he said. "Gold is a precious metal. It's so precious that you can trade it for things you want."

"Like honey?" Pooh couldn't help saying.

"I suppose," said Owl, trying to be patient.

And so it was that Owl, Pooh, Tigger, and Roo went in search of the pot at the end of the rainbow.

As the friends hurried through the forest, hoping that the rainbow wouldn't disappear before they found the gold, they ran into Piglet.

"Hello, Piglet," said Pooh. "We're searching for a pot of gold."

"Gold's shiny," Roo chimed in, "and more precious than honey!"

Piglet was disappointed. "Oh," he said, "you probably won't want to share it, then."

"Nonsense," said Pooh.

"The more the merrier," said Owl. "For all we know, there's a *huge* pot of gold just waiting for all of us!"

As the friends hurried along, Piglet asked, "Pooh, do you know where the end of the rainbow is?"

"No," said Pooh. "I was following you."

"But I was following Roo," said Piglet.

Roo pointed at Tigger. "But I was following him," the little kangaroo said.

"From up here," Owl called down to them, "the rainbow looks like it ends at Poohsticks Bridge."

Suddenly Piglet noticed something shiny beneath a tree. "Oh!" he cried. "I found the gold!"

Piglet's friends eagerly hurried over to the glittering object and gathered around.

"I'm sorry, Piglet," said Owl, "but I'm afraid what we have here is not a pot of gold but, well, a — rock."

Pooh saw that Piglet was embarrassed. "But it's a very nice rock," he said kindly. "Here, Piglet. You keep it."

"Thank you," Piglet said, taking the rock in his hand. The sunlight glinted off some shiny flecks all over its surface.

"Why, it *is* nice," Piglet said cheerfully. "I think I'll put it on my dresser."

They continued on their way. After a while, Tigger felt a crunch beneath his feet.

"Oops," he said. "I stepped on something."

The others glanced at the ground.

"Oh, dear," said Piglet. "You stepped on a robin's egg."

"Yes, but it's empty," Pooh announced happily. "Look, here are more empty shells. The babies must have hatched and flown away with their mother."

"Look at what a bright blue these eggs are!" said
Tigger. "They even have speckles on them — like someone
splashed them with paint!"

"They are pretty, aren't they?" said Pooh.
"Yup, and I'm going to take one home with me,"
said Tigger. "That blue makes me feel all bouncy!"

But Roo was more interested in the nest in the grass. "May I keep it?" he asked.

"Since the robins are finished with it, I don't see why not," said Owl.

And so, carefully carrying their newfound treasures, the friends continued their search for the pot of gold.

As they approached Poohsticks Bridge, Roo looked up and said, "Uh-oh! The rainbow's disappearing!"

"Hurry, everyone!" Owl cried. "Spread out and look for the pot of gold! There's no time to lose!"

Owl flew across the bridge and began searching on the other side. Tigger, Roo, and Piglet put down what they were carrying and scrambled down the bank. Pooh ran to the middle of the bridge and looked at the water below, just in case the pot of gold had fallen in.

After a moment, Pooh cried, "Roo! Do you see something by the bridge?"

"It's a pot!" Roo called excitedly.

Owl hurried over as Pooh ran across the bridge, then slid down the bank.

When Pooh reached his friends, he saw disappointed looks on all their faces. Then he saw the pot. It was not full of gold, but full of honey.

"Oh!" Pooh cried happily. "It's number three!"
"Number three?" muttered Owl, frowning.

"Yes," Pooh continued. "It's my missing honey pot. I was counting my honey pots this morning, and I only had two. This is number three."

"But what is it doing *here*?" a grumpy Owl asked.
"I left it here yesterday," Pooh explained. "I must have forgotten it when I packed up my picnic things."

"I know we didn't find the pot of gold," Piglet declared brightly, "but we collected lots of treasures — like this shiny rock."

"And some bright blue robin's eggs," said Tigger.

"And a wonderful nest," said Roo.

"*And* my missing honey pot," said Pooh, grinning.

"Hmmph," Owl grumbled. "That may be well and good for *you*, but *I* didn't find anything."

All at once, Pooh had an idea. He took honey pot number three and tipped it upside down until he had eaten every last bit of honey inside.

"Wait here," he said, hurrying into the woods.

A short while later he returned, his honey pot overflowing with red, blue, green, and yellow berries.

"You may not have found a pot of gold at the end of the rainbow, but now you have your very own rainbow *in* a pot of gold," said Pooh proudly.

"So I do," said Owl, admiring the beautiful rainbow-colored berries in the golden-colored pot before him.